Laughing on Butterfly Wings

AND OTHER STORIES OF LONG AGO

Compiled by the Editors
of
Highlights for Children

Published by Highlights for Children, Inc.
P.O. Box 18201
Columbus, Ohio 43218-0201
Printed in the United States of America

ISBN 0-87534-660-X

CONTENTS

Laughing on Butterfly Wings

By Lee Ebler

Sara and I were walking home through the fields. We had been picking beans for Aunt Jo. Picking was hot work in August, but Aunt Jo paid twenty cents a bushel, and that was good money on Sourwood Road.

Sara had already spent her first week's pay.

"I bought a new bonnet," she said. "And then I got Annie a butterfly pin. Something to remember me by forever."

We were quiet for a minute. The only sound was the *swoosh* of our calico skirts as they trailed over the grasses. We were both thinking of Annie, who was moving West with her family in a covered wagon. Annie loved butterflies.

"It's a small present so Annie can take it with her," Sara said. I wished I could have bought Annie a town-made gift. But my bean-picking money went for kerosene and other necessities.

"What are you bringing to the going-away party, Kate?" Sara asked me.

It wasn't really a party, but our neighbors were getting together to say good-bye to Annie and her folks. And they were bringing presents—small treasures that would fit in the covered wagon. My ma was sending a jar of her best watermelon pickles.

"I want to give Annie a gift that will make her laugh again," I said. "She's been sad since she found out she was leaving. But I can't find a present special enough."

"You're not bringing anything?" Sara asked, sounding surprised.

"I guess not. It's too late now," I replied.

"You could make her a present real quick," Sara said. "Knit her something."

I shook my head. The only thing I could knit

were wool scarves, and they always unraveled. Besides, no one wants a wool scarf in August.

Sara and I parted at Buttermilk Creek, and I walked on alone to our farm. It was a warm afternoon. The corn was standing tall in the fields, and Ma's flower garden was full of bees, butterflies, and sunshine.

I liked Ma's garden, so I sat for a while on my favorite rock, watching butterflies sip nectar from flowers. I thought about how I would miss Annie. I hoped there were butterflies out West for her.

I wished I could give her a package of butterflies to open along the way. I pictured butterflies drifting out of the covered wagon like a trail of smoke. Annie could be the Johnny Appleseed of butterflies.

I thought very hard, and then I ran into the house to find Ma. I'd had my first butterfly idea. Ma thought it was a good one.

"I'll show you which ones to pick," she said. "And I'll write out directions."

So I had my special gift for Annie. On the way to the party, I had another butterfly brainstorm.

Most of the neighbors were visiting in the yard, but Annie and Sara were waiting for me in the kitchen. The kitchen was sad and bare because the furniture had been sold. Annie was on the floor, wearing Sara's pin, and she was trying not to cry.

"Oh, Kate. I was afraid you wouldn't come," Annie said. "I was afraid I'd never see you again!"

"Of course I came," I said. "And I've got two presents for you."

"You had time to make two presents?" Sara said. "They're not going to unravel, are they?"

"Come and see," I said.

We left the house, and I led them down the path to the low spot near Buttermilk Creek. Then I made them close their eyes, while I led them over the footbridge.

"Ouch!" Sara said, tripping. "Watch where I'm going, Kate!"

Annie didn't say anything, but she squeezed my hand hard.

"You can look now!" I said and heard both Annie and Sara gasp. The clearing around the bridge was filled with butterflies, beautiful monarch butterflies, floating like flakes of orange and black snow.

"My ma says they're migrating," I said. "They like this spot because of the milkweeds. Milkweeds make the monarchs bitter-tasting so the birds won't eat them."

Annie looked and looked. She held up her arms, and the butterflies brushed against her and landed in her hair. They swirled and danced above us.

"I wish I could take all this with me," Annie said at last.

And that was when I brought out the package Ma had helped me fix.

"Here are special flower seeds," I said. "Plant them in your new garden, and Ma says they'll attract butterflies."

"What a wonderful present!" Annie said. Then she threw back her head and laughed, really laughed. The laughter was so happy that Sara and I joined her.

And in the silence that followed, I think I heard the sound of butterfly wings.

The Hobo Camp

By Nancy Day

The best part of our Saturday walks was when my father and I would stop by the old hobo camp. The camp is less than a mile from my father's boyhood home in Belvidere, Illinois. We'd walk across East Pleasant Street to the railroad tracks, then follow the rails out of town, along the Kishwaukee River.

Near the milepost, my father would point to a bare spot among some trees beside the river. "There's where the hobo camp used to be," he'd say.

"But there's nothing there," I'd reply, just to get him started. My father would smile, take me by the hand, and we'd slide sideways down the steep riverbank for a closer look. As we sat under a tree and watched the water glide by, my dad would start to tell his stories, and the old hobo camp stirred to life. . . .

The 1930s were rough years. Dad was a boy then, and he lived in a small farmhouse covered with tar paper. The country was in a depression, and money was hard to come by. Many people lost their jobs and their money. Some of them became hoboes.

Hoboes jumped aboard freight trains and rode from town to town, looking for work. Hobo camps sprung up along the railroad lines, usually near sources of fresh water. Men with names like Windmill Blacky, Scoop Shovel Scotty, and Fry Pan Jack stopped at the camps to eat, sleep, tell stories, and share dreams.

Belvidere had a railroad and a river, so it was a good place to camp. After hoboes made camp, they might head into town to find work and food. They often knocked on the back door of my father's house and asked if they could work for a meal. My father's mother—my grandmother—usually couldn't think of any work for the hoboes, but she gave them meals anyway. She would load up plates with whatever she had and serve them on the back porch.

Of the stories my father tells, my favorite is the one about Hairbreadth Harry. But to hear that one, you have to hear about Murph first. Murph was my father's hobo friend. Most of the hoboes Dad met came and went with the trains. Murph didn't. He lived at the hobo camp. He had built himself a cabin out of old railroad ties and scraps of wood. He even wrote an address—1313 Riverside Avenue—over the door.

My dad and his friend Joe used to stop by 1313 Riverside Avenue on their way to their special fishing spot. They would sit with the hoboes and listen to their stories. Sometimes Murph would play the harmonica. When mealtime came, the hoboes shared any food they had. This usually included whatever fish they'd caught in the Kishwaukee that day. They cooked everything over a big open fire, right there on the riverbank.

Before long one of the hoboes would announce, "I think I'll go south for a while." Another would say, "I'm going to catch the next train to Chicago." The next day, only Murph would be left.

One day, Murph told my father that an honored guest was at the hobo camp. Then he presented

Hairbreadth Harry, King of the Hoboes. It turned out there had been a hobo convention somewhere in Iowa. Hoboes had traveled from all over the country to meet, and they elected Hairbreadth Harry as king.

Hairbreadth Harry had been born in Belvidere. He had been roaming since he was twenty-four years old and was older than fifty when my dad met him. He wore sandals that were just boards tied to his feet. My father remembered the flapping noise they made when he walked.

Hairbreadth Harry had been all over, but he'd never seen a hobo camp quite like 1313 Riverside Avenue. He listened to Murph's harmonica, shared stories, and told strange poems that he made up on the spot.

Hairbreadth Harry stayed for a few days. Then he was gone.

Murph is gone now, too, as are the other hoboes. The cabin at 1313 Riverside Avenue no longer stands. The bare spot by the river is all that remains. But my father still remembers. And when we sit on the shore of the Kishwaukee, I close my eyes and hear the sweet sound of Murph's harmonica, smell the fresh fish sizzling over the fire, and see Hairbreadth Harry's wild sandals flip-flapping along the riverbank.

Papa's Return

By Elizabeth Weiss Vollstadt

Eunice Pinkham wasn't at all happy, but no one noticed. Papa's ship had been sighted, and everyone was getting ready for his return.

Mama sent Eunice to the storage cellar three times: first for some sweet potatoes; then to get a winter squash; then for jars of preserves, each carefully labeled "Beach Plum, Summer 1840."

"Just think," she said to Eunice, "your papa's ship will be in Nantucket Harbor by nightfall.

And then your papa will be home at last." There was a new melody in her voice as she talked.

Twelve-year-old Jonathan whistled as he chopped wood outside the kitchen door. Even Eunice's sister, Mary, who was almost a grown-up at fourteen, hummed to herself as she swept and dusted the parlor.

"What fun we'll have when Papa's home," she told Eunice. "He tells stories of faraway places—like islands where it never snows—and plays all kinds of games with us. You used to laugh and laugh when he lifted you high over his head. Don't you remember?"

But Eunice didn't remember anything about Papa. He was the captain of a whaling ship and had been gone for over three years—ever since she was two years old. She wasn't at all sure she would like having a stranger in their house.

"Eunice!" It was Mama calling again. She ran quickly to the kitchen.

Mama was cutting up the winter squash. "Would you go to Silas Mott's store for me?" she asked. "He said he was going clamming this morning and would bring some back for us. Maybe I can make your papa's favorite chowder."

Eunice felt very grown up as she made her way down the cobblestones of Main Street. Mama hardly ever let her walk into town all by herself.

She reached Mr. Mott's store just as a tall man with dark eyes and a black beard burst through the door. He was frowning and muttering angrily over his shoulder, "We'll see about that."

Mr. Mott called after him. "But, Mr. Pinkham . . . "

The man pushed past Eunice. "Out of my way," he growled.

Eunice stared after him, her eyes open wide. Mr. Mott had called the angry man "Mr. Pinkham." He must be Papa! Two big tears welled up in her eyes. She didn't feel grown up anymore. Why did Papa have to come home anyway?

She walked slowly into the store. Mr. Mott called a cheery, "You may take a piece of candy while I get the clams." But even the sweet taste of maple sugar didn't make her feel better.

A few minutes later, Eunice had the package of clams clutched tightly in her arms. She wished she didn't have to go home now. What would she do if Papa was there already, yelling at Mama because the chowder wasn't ready?

The walk up Main Street seemed much too short. When she got home, Mary was waiting on the porch. She was almost dancing with impatience.

"Quick, Eunice," she said. "Mama and Jonathan have taken the shortcut to the harbor. The winds were good and Papa's ship has docked already. Let me quickly put these clams away, and then we can go, too."

Mary took the package from Eunice. Then her eyes opened wide as she glanced down the street. "Papa!" she yelled. Dropping the package of clams, she raced down the street toward a bearded man. He looked like the man Eunice had seen storming out of Mr. Mott's store.

Eunice knew she didn't want to see him again. Heart pounding, she ran up the wooden stairs. Where could she hide? She raced over to the small clothes cupboard in the room she shared with Mary. Maybe if she stayed very still, no one would find her.

But moments later, she heard heavy footsteps clumping up the stairs. "Where's my Eunice?" a deep voice said. "Could she be behind the silk screen from my voyage to Japan? I remember her playing there."

Eunice said nothing. The footsteps came closer and the voice boomed again. "Could she be behind the chest from China?" The voice didn't sound as mean as the voice in Mr. Mott's store, but Eunice could picture the frowning face. She stayed very still.

The heavy footsteps came into her room. *Clump. Clump.* Closer. Closer.

"Or is she in the cupboard made right here in Nantucket?" The door opened slowly. Eunice shrank back as far as she could. "Well, what have we here?" asked the voice.

There was no way out. Eunice lifted her head and looked up—right into a pair of smiling blue eyes. It wasn't the man from the store at all!

"You're not Papa," she cried. "I saw Papa at Mr. Mott's store. He was angry and mean."

She stopped, frightened by her own daring. But the man with the blue eyes just threw back his head and laughed.

"Of course I'm your papa," he said finally. "I would wager that you ran into my brother Reuben, just off the ship, too." He kneeled down to look directly into Eunice's eyes. His voice grew soft. "Reuben is a nasty fellow. I would have hidden, too, if I thought he were my papa."

He opened his arms. Some distant memory stirred deep inside Eunice, and she went into his hug. Then, big as she was, Papa stood up and lifted her high over his head. She looked into his blue eyes and they laughed together.

No-Man's-Land

By Susan Campbell Bartoletti

Micah Jenkins cracked open the leather-bound diary his ma had given him before he marched out of Oglethorpe last spring. *November 30, 1862,* he wrote. *We still await orders. Our regiment had one extra drill for making sport of the drummer. Went on picket duty.*

Micah sighed as he slipped the diary into his haversack. More than once older soldiers had told him that a fourteen-year-old boy should be home, waiting for whiskers to sprout. Instead, here he stood near the Rappahannock River, guarding against the tinkling of cowbells and other calls that could turn into Yankee scouts.

"Hello, Reb!" came a call across the stream.

"Hello, Yank," answered Jules, another Rebel picket stationed near Micah.

"We're getting water."

"Go ahead. We won't look."

Micah recognized the voice. It belonged to the Yankee whom he had met earlier as they both gathered firewood from the same rail fence. The boy couldn't have been any older than Micah. *Now we'll be drinking from opposite sides of the same stream,* he thought.

After a few splashes, the Yankee called again, "Hey, Reb."

"Yeah?" Micah replied.

"We left a little something for your trouble."

The brush crackled as the Union soldiers left. Micah ran to the water's edge and plucked a small, crudely built boat from the reeds. He took out coffee and nuts. The other pickets whooped with joy and took turns sniffing the coffee beans.

"Seems strange to have Yanks camped so close," said Micah.

"After Malvern Hill my regiment fell upon some Yankees picking blueberries," said Jules.

"What happened?" asked Micah.

Jules chuckled. "We called our own truce and spent the morning picking berries together." He paused, then added, "Of course, we picked more than they did."

"We've sneaked across picket lines to play cards with Yanks," said Charley. "Beat them every time."

"That's nothing," said Goodloe. "Once we held a swimming party with a company of Bluecoats. There's nothing uglier than a white-bellied Yankee—unless it's a blue-bellied one."

As the pickets laughed, Micah wished he had something to give the Yanks, but all his haversack held was his diary, a mess kit, a jackknife, a mending kit, and a ball of darning yarn.

Suddenly he had an idea. He took a Minié ball from the ammunition box and wound his darning yarn tightly around it until he had a yarn ball as big as his fist. Then he knotted the ends of the yarn. On a piece of paper he scrawled "good sport" and pinned it to the ball.

He ran down to the water. "Hey, Yank," he called. "Here's something for you."

The bushes rustled, then the young Yankee appeared on the bank. Micah tossed the ball across. The Yankee caught it and smiled as he read the note.

"We've got a hickory rail for a bat," said the Yankee. "How many good sports are there in that sorry-looking camp of yours?"

"Enough to give you the best whupping you ever got," Goodloe hollered.

The Yankees laughed, and a harmonica sang out "Yankee Doodle." Charley's harmonica retaliated with a chorus of "Dixie."

The next day the Rebels and the Yankees faced each other in "No-Man's-Land," a narrow clearing that lay between the lines. Behind each team the flags were hoisted high. Between them, the white flag of truce fluttered.

Gripping the yarn ball, Micah eyed the Yankee's hickory-rail bat and pitched the ball. *Crack!* A Rebel scooped up the ball and aimed for the Yankee. Too late. The Yank was safe at first.

By the third inning, the Yankees led, 23-22, with Jules on second base. Both sides groaned as they saw that the yarn ball had unraveled to a pile of thread.

"Find a rock," suggested Goodloe.

"Here, Reb," a Yankee yelled, tossing a walnut-sized rock in the air. A Rebel wadded the yarn around the rock. Another Yankee peeled off his sock and dropped the yarn-and-rock wadding into it. Cheering, the teams quickly fell into their places.

The hickory rail felt splintery in Micah's hands as he stood, feet planted and eyes locked on the pitcher. The Yankee tossed the sock-ball. Micah swung. *Whack!* His heart pounding, he tagged first base, then on to second. Jules rounded third base, then sped for home. Dirt flying, he slid into home, tying the score at 23. Shouts and cheers rang out.

Micah tensed, ready to run as the next batter faced the pitcher, but just as the pitcher brought his arm back, the Rebel bugle sounded, calling the men to formation. As the white flag was lowered, Micah's eyes met the Yankee's who had caught the yarn ball across the stream. The two boys raised their hands in salute, then quietly followed the men from "No-Man's-Land."

That night camp fires lit the fields like fallen stars. Micah listened as the Yankees across the stream sang "Home Sweet Home." One by one, the Rebels joined in.

Micah wrote in his diary, *December 1, 1862. Reinforcements have arrived. We're ordered to keep in readiness all night.*

Belinda

By Connie Elliott

Nancy stood with her family in the stable yard. Her father had hitched the horses to the wagon and was ready to leave.

"How long will you be gone, Pa?" she asked.

"About a week," said Mr. Parker. He was traveling from their home on the Texas plains out to where the trees grew. There he would load up on firewood.

"I think you could get back faster if you'd take Henry with you," said Nancy. Henry was Nancy's older brother.

Mr. Parker frowned. "We've been all through that. It's almost time for the baby to be born. If anything happens while I'm away, Henry can ride for Dr. Harris."

"I can ride for Doc Harris," Nancy said.

"Ha! You're always dreaming with your head in the clouds," said Henry.

"I am not!"

"Hush, both of you," said Ma. "No one is going to have to ride for Doc Harris. The baby won't be born for another month."

Pa hugged each of the children and his wife, then he drove away in the cool morning light.

Ma went inside, and Henry and little Wesley went off to feed the one remaining horse. Nancy continued to watch as the wagon rumbled down the dirt road. She climbed partway up the windmill and watched as the cloud of dust got farther away.

The flat prairie stretched as far as she could see. Only a few windmills marked the scattered farms. It was the only country Nancy had ever seen. Ma and Pa had told the children about the green hills of Kentucky, but Nancy hadn't even been born yet when her parents left there.

Sometimes Nancy dreamed of living in a big white house surrounded by green lawns. She would wear a long blue dress with puffed sleeves and a big collar. Her name would be Belinda. She had seen that name in a book once.

"Nancy, come here, please." Ma's voice interrupted her daydream.

Nancy went inside. A piece of red fabric was spread on the table.

"School will be starting again soon," Ma said. "Would you like to have a new red dress?"

Nancy touched the cloth. "It's pretty. Could I have a big collar and puffed sleeves?" *A Belinda dress*, she thought.

"You sure can," Ma said.

The next morning, the children were busy gathering beans, carrots, and onions. They carried the tubs of vegetables inside. Nancy's heart sank when she saw how many beans there were. They would be canning for days.

"Henry, I promised Mrs. Sanders that I would send her some of these beans," Ma said. "The bugs got to theirs. Why don't you ride over this afternoon and take them a bag of these."

"But I told Pa I'd stay here with you," he said.

Nancy hoped that Henry wouldn't have one of his stubborn spells. She hoped he would take a big bag of those beans away.

"I'll be fine," Ma said. "And I know that you'll be back by suppertime."

Henry grinned. "I'll go."

Nancy, Wesley, and Ma went to work snapping beans. After a while, Ma stood and rubbed her back. "I'm going to lie down. Keep an eye on Wesley," she said to Nancy.

Nancy and Wesley kept snapping beans, but Nancy couldn't stop thinking about Ma. She couldn't remember a time when Ma ever had to lay down in the middle of the day . . . except when Wesley was born.

"Oh no," she said.

"What's wrong?" Wesley asked.

"Nothing. I'll be right back." She tiptoed to her mother's room. Ma's eyes were closed. "Is it time for the baby to come?" Nancy whispered.

"I think so," said Ma. "Don't worry. There's plenty of time."

"I'll get help," said Nancy.

"No. You have to look after Wesley. Promise me you won't leave."

Nancy gulped. "I promise."

She hurried outside and climbed the windmill to look up the road, hoping Henry would be on his way back. But there was no cloud of dust. He wasn't coming.

Nancy searched the horizon. Far in the distance, there seemed to be someone on the road.

Nancy waved her arms. "Help!" she hollered. But she knew her voice wouldn't carry so far.

Suddenly she had an idea. She scrambled down the windmill and raced to the house. She quickly grabbed the red dress Ma had been working on and raced back outside.

Nancy hurried up the windmill and tied the dress to one of the blades. She pulled. The windmill began turning, with the red dress flying in the breeze. Nancy turned the windmill again and again until her arms ached.

The wheel creaked to a stop. The dress hung there, limp and dusty.

Nancy's arms and legs felt like stones as she lowered herself to the ground. She leaned against the windmill and closed her eyes.

It was a stupid idea, she thought. *Maybe Henry was right. Maybe my head is always in the clouds.*

Just then she heard something, and she strained her ears to hear. A rumbling wagon was approaching through the dust. The wagon carried Mr. and Mrs. Martin from the next farm over.

Nancy cried tears of relief as she explained. Mrs. Martin went in to help Ma, and Mr. Martin rode to get the doctor. By evening, Ma had given birth to a daughter.

Pa arrived home a few days later, and he burst into a smile as he picked up the baby. "Sure glad I left Henry home," he said.

"Nancy got help, Pa," said Henry. He quickly told Pa the story.

"Well, I'll be switched," Pa said. He grinned at Nancy. "I guess I needn't worry when I'm away."

"That's right," said Ma. She put her arm around Nancy. "Now we need a name for this baby. Do you have any ideas, Nancy?"

Nancy already knew the perfect name. "Let's call her Belinda."

The rest of the family talked it over. They agreed that Belinda Parker was a fine name.

Miss Pendergast and the Wolves

By G.M. Glass

Our first schoolteacher was supposed to come from a neighboring town. But when word came that he had been kicked by a mule, somebody sent all the way to Boston for Miss Pendergast.

In late summer she moved into the small log cabin a few miles from our Montana town. The new schoolhouse was just a holler away from her cabin.

Her crated-up furniture was unloaded from the weekly train and piled onto the blacksmith's wagon: a green velvet sofa, small spindly-legged tables with animal paws carved on the bottoms, chairs covered with green and gold satin, tall chests, and boxes and boxes of books.

Folks decided right off that Miss Pendergast was a lady of quality. But what she was doing teaching the children of Montana homesteaders stayed her private business.

I was twelve, and school was the last place I wanted to be. Thoughts of being a sailor, soldier, or mountain man filled my head. My mother had been teaching me since I was little, so I wasn't pure ignorant. Just satisfied that I already knew enough.

That first morning in the one-room schoolhouse I met a little gray-haired lady who stood and walked ramrod straight, as though she had a yard-stick nailed to her back. By noon I was feeling mighty sorry for her.

The Johnson boys wouldn't mind a word she said. At lunchtime they pinched whatever they wanted from our lunch pails. Since they were a head or more taller than the rest of us, everybody suffered in silence.

That same afternoon Miss Pendergast announced that there would be no school till further notice. We learned later that she had sent a note to Mr. Johnson, the boys' father.

The next day my mother sent me to the teacher's house with an apple pie. I was in the built-on shed, filling the woodbox, when Mr. Johnson rode up on his chestnut mare.

Call it eavesdropping if you like, but I froze, listening. Mr. Johnson was known to be a considerable hard man.

I heard Miss Pendergast tell him how unruly his boys were. And if this continued, she said, she'd resign. And when the school board wanted to know why, she would tell them it was because Mr. Johnson couldn't get his sons to behave. Now, if he wanted everyone in the territory to know that his boys had no respect for their own father, he certainly had her sympathy.

I grinned when I heard that bear of a man promising a big change. And would she *please*, he said, not even think about leaving.

School got better after that.

Winter came hard that year, bringing dark, storm-filled days and nights. Cutting, blinding snows piled up in thirty-foot drifts. Roads disappeared. Houses were buried. Cattle and horses froze standing up. For three days folks huddled in their homes. Then came the freeze: six more days of a cold so harsh that water froze in kitchen jugs.

Finally, the freeze was over. The men dug the snow away from blocked doors and hurried to help their neighbors. I begged my father to let me go check on Miss Pendergast. We strapped on our snowshoes and set out.

Four hours later, stiff with the cold, we saw a white wall with only the top of a chimney showing. All around were wolf tracks. They went clear up to the roof.

I was the first to see a sign of life. "Pa, smoke just came out of the chimney!" I called.

I helped clear away the snow, all the time thinking, *Please don't let her be frozen in her bed*. Then the door slowly opened.

"Gentlemen, how good to see you," said Miss Pendergast. She was terrible pale. We stepped inside and saw a bare cabin.

Miss Pendergast shrugged, and smiled weakly. "I burned almost everything," she said, "once the woodbox was empty."

While standing there, I felt an icy-cold draft touch my head. I glanced up and spied a patch of blue sky through a four-inch hole in the roof. The wolves had gnawed right through. The beams by the hole were scorched black where Miss Pendergast must have been waving a torch. She probably burned those fancy table legs. I wondered how long it had been since she slept, what with those hungry wolves worrying around, trying to get in.

"They weren't coming after you, ma'am. Wolves don't attack people. I expect they were after that," said my father, pointing to a frozen slab of bacon hanging inside by the woodshed.

"Your books, Miss Pendergast. You could have burned them next," I offered cheerfully.

"Burn my books? I should say not!" she said, looking right at me. "They're my magic carpet to all the wonderful places of the world, to seas I've never sailed and people I've never known."

"The floorboards were next," she added, nodding at a hatchet standing against one wall.

There were more storms that winter, but none were as bad. Every day I walked the teacher home. It was me who taught Miss Pendergast how to load, fire, and clean her new rifle, so she could defend herself.

Before long I found myself stretched out on the floor, reading her books, one after the other.

Then one day she told me, "Matthew, you remind me so much of young Mr. Lincoln, reading there by the light of the fire."

Me and Abe Lincoln? Imagine that! Me and Abe Lincoln.

Caroline's Gift

By Gina T. Reitman

One night an old woman lay in bed, writing a letter to the girl who lived next door. Often the girl had come to the house with her mother, who helped the old woman with her cooking and cleaning. Thinking the old woman took too much of her mother's time, the girl often scowled and grumbled. They had never spoken to each other.

With a wobbly hand, the old woman scribbled the girl's name on an envelope. She pinned it atop a folded quilt and smiled. Later that night, she died.

The pastor from the old woman's church brought the quilt and the letter to the girl. With her mother beside her, the girl began to read.

Dear Child,

I'm so old—nearly ninety-four. Where all those years went, I don't know. Everyone dear to me is gone. I had no children. Some would say that I had a sad life, and maybe that's partways true, but it had its moments.

The quilt is for you. It tells a story about my mother and me. I stitched it long ago from the very clothes we wore on an April night in 1910 when a truly wondrous thing occurred. I was just about the age you are now.

Back then we were alone up here on the hill—no other houses, no neighbors. Town was two miles away, and the only way down was by foot or by mule. But we weren't lonely, for we had plenty of work tending the chickens and the garden. I had my schooling, and Mama took in sewing. And we had each other.

On that day in April, I was throwing apple peelings to the chickens when I first saw Mama looking up. She shaded her eyes with her hand and searched the sky. I found myself looking, too, but I saw nothing. When I asked what she was doing, she said I'd know soon enough. Then she went inside the house. I could hear her through the window, flipping the pages of a book.

We had a great many books, for Mama was a reader. She said we'd never have the means to see the world in person, but we could see it all through the words of others.

The previous September we had traded four sacks of walnuts for a used encyclopedia. Mama considered us rich after that.

That afternoon we were pulling dandelion weeds in the garden when Mama did it again. Kneeling in the damp soil, her face all lit by the sun, she squinted up at the sky.

"Mama, what are you looking at?" I asked.

"It won't be in our world, Caroline," she said, her eyes still staring heavenward. Then she took my face in her hands. "Be patient, child. I want to give you something special—a gift you'll not get again in your life. Let me do that."

"Of course, Mama," I said, and she pulled me tight against her.

When the first star appeared, Mama went to collect the firewood from the side of the chicken coop. I saw her gazing into the brilliant blue night, shaking her head. Passing me on the porch, she sighed. "I felt so sure it would have come by now."

Mama made me a bed before the fire and read from the encyclopedia, covering subjects from the Civil War to Coronado. I listened to the hiss of the damp wood burning and the crackle of book pages turning. I quickly fell asleep.

When I woke, the room was dark and cold and the fire nearly gone. Mama was nudging my arm.

"What time is it?" I asked in a voice hoarse with sleep. "Where are we going?" Mama didn't answer as she led me into the night.

"It's come, Caroline," she said. Her breath was like smoke in the air. "We'll walk to the ridge. You can see it from there."

I stumbled behind her in the dark as beetles and field mice bolted for their burrows. We came from behind the tall oaks into a clearing.

"There! You see?" Mama said, pointing skyward. Perhaps my eyes were clouded with sleep, for I saw nothing. I turned to Mama, and there, reflected in her eyes, I saw it—a bright ball of light trailing a misty tail across the sky.

"What is it, Mama?" I asked.

"It's Halley's comet," she said. "Unless you grow very old, you'll never see it again. It passes earth but once every seventy-five years." Mama reached for my cold hand. I could feel the blood pounding in her palm.

"More than two thousand years ago, this very thing we're looking at was seen by a Roman ruler named Julius Caesar. He was fourteen years old and terrified. Everyone was terrified. For ages people thought comets caused disease and war and deaths of kings."

Mama turned her gaze to the bluff's highest point. "Come on, Caroline," she said. "We're going to the top." Without another word, she dropped my hand and began to climb.

I scrambled after her, with leaves and twigs snapping under our feet. "But what is it really?" I yelled up at her. "Where did it come from?"

"It orbits the sun," she called, never slowing her pace. "It's made of gases and dust but mostly plain old ice. It's like nothing so much as a giant, dirty snowball. The only difference is that it's millions of years old."

My legs were tired. I yelled to Mama, "I have to catch my breath." I sat on a bed of leaves. Mama walked back to join me.

She was breathing hard but the words kept coming. "People simply hadn't the facts in days past. They thought Halley's comet was an evil omen . . . a sign of God's fury or a trick of the devil's."

I felt my strength returning, and we began to climb again. "Almost there now," Mama said. I inched toward the edge of the bluff and looked down. I could see the river sparkling in the valley below. Then I looked up. The comet seemed even brighter.

Suddenly a gust of wind raced over the bluff, and I shivered. Mama hugged me. Her hair was flying back from her face. In the comet's light her skin looked like fine, white marble.

"All those kings and queens and emperors through the centuries have looked upon this very thing," Mama said. "And now you and I are looking on it, too." She held me away from her and stared into my eyes. "I can't give you much, Caroline. But I can give you this." Then she turned again to the sky. "It's my gift to you."

"It's a real sight, Mama," I said.

We were quiet then. Chickadees began to chirp in the pines, signaling the coming of morning. We stayed on the bluff until the sky began to lighten. When we turned for home, I could hear the rooster calling from the yard.

Mama was right. I never did see Halley's comet again, though I certainly lived long enough. It passed earth about eight years ago. But by then my vision was poor, and the nights were cloudy. I strained to see but couldn't. Perhaps it doesn't matter. Halley's comet could never again be as bright as that night when I was just a girl. Some things happen only once.

I feel myself weakening, but I'm at ease. I've told my tale and now I'll sleep. This quilt was stitched from the very clothes we wore that night in 1910. It's my gift to you.

With much affection,
Caroline Wesley

Slowly the girl folded the letter, then unfolded the quilt. It showed a glorious star-filled night with a big white ball dashing across the sky. The girl traced its path with her finger. She asked if she could see where Caroline was buried. Though night was near, her mother agreed. In the yard the girl picked wild lilies to lay on the old woman's grave.

The moon had risen by the time they reached the cemetery. Through the trees, it dotted their path with silvery light. They found the grave where the oaks were tall and thick and moss grew on the rocks. She was buried beside her mother. They shared one gravestone. The girl stepped over and read the words aloud:

Margaret Anne Wesley
1882-1916
Caroline Maude Wesley
1899-1993

Gently the girl set the lilies between them. When she turned, she saw her mother staring up at the sky. The girl could see the stars shining in her mother's eyes.

TWO OLD FRIENDS

By Laura E. Hill

Daniel McGee listened as the wind howled across the snow-covered cornfields. The wood around his window groaned and creaked with each icy blast. In the next room, his newborn baby sister, Virginia, slept in a handmade cradle.

A wood-burning furnace provided the McGee home with warmth—the warmth necessary to keep a newborn baby well. But with all the excitement of the baby coming, no one had noticed that the woodpile had grown dangerously low. Now Father would have to go to the timber to get more wood. Since Daniel was nine years old, he would be going, too. He had waited a very long time for this day.

Daniel and his father put on their heaviest coats and boots and made their way to the barn. Once inside, Father harnessed Sam and Joe, the two black mules, to the wagon. At first they resisted and Father became irritated.

"First thing next week these stubborn creatures are goin' to the glue factory," he said. "I can't afford to keep animals that have outlived their usefulness."

Daniel didn't say a word. He understood how his father felt, but hoped he would change his mind. Sam and Joe were like old friends to Daniel. They had taught him to ride.

Father cracked his whip in the crisp air. The sound made an eerie echo. As he drove the wagon across the open fields, the full force of the wind struck. The wind made it hard for them to breathe, so they bent their heads until their chins touched their chests. Now they could barely see where they were going. Thank goodness Sam and Joe knew the way to the timber by heart.

When they finally reached the timber, Father stopped the wagon and tied the mules to a tree. Then he grabbed a saw and looked for the best trees to cut down. Not too green and not too old, Daniel remembered.

Before long, two trees were lying on the forest floor. Daniel helped Father cut them into sections and load them into the wagon.

"One more tree ought to do the job, son," said Father. "Stand clear now."

Daniel stood back and watched his father make the final cuts on a nearby tree. When he was done, Father gave the tree a shove. Nothing happened. He tried again. Still nothing.

Then Father had an idea. He untied the mules and backed the wagon under the tree. Maybe, if he stood in the wagon, he would have better luck. He would be up higher and could push from a different place on the trunk. He figured it was worth a try, so he climbed onto the wagon and stood on the driver's seat.

As Father reached for the tree, Daniel heard the sound of splitting wood. Without any warning, the tree started falling toward his father! With a crash, the enormous trunk fell to the side of the wagon. Snow from the tree filled the air. When it cleared, Daniel could see a large branch sprawled across the spot where his father had been standing. His father, knocked into the wagon by the branch, lay silent and still.

Daniel rushed to his father. There was a large wound on Father's head, and blood was streaming down his face. He took a handkerchief from his pocket and placed it on his father's wound. Then he pressed down hard to try and stop the bleeding. It seemed to help. The boy pushed and pulled, but he couldn't budge the branch.

Daniel tied the mules to the wagon. He knew it was up to him to get his father home. But how could he drive the wagon and tend to his father at the same time? If he left Father alone in the wagon on the bumpy ride home, Daniel was afraid his father would lose too much blood.

And what about the branch? He couldn't go anywhere until the branch was off the wagon.

As Daniel tried to think of a solution, he felt the wagon move. Suddenly, it lurched forward. Daniel sat up and saw that the mules were trying to move the wagon! They tried for several minutes and snorted loudly with each attempt. Then they stopped, exhausted.

"Come on, boys! You can do it!" yelled Daniel.

But the mules didn't move. Now Daniel became anxious. "You useless old mules. Maybe you deserve to go to the glue factory after all!" he cried.

The mules lowered their heads, and then using every muscle in their strong bodies, tried again.

This time they jerked the wagon so forcefully that the branch went sailing off the wagon. Finally free of their cumbersome load, the mules were now able to make their way home. Since they knew the way so well, Daniel didn't need to drive. He stayed with Father the whole way home.

The mules got them home that afternoon. And after several days, Father was feeling much better. Then Daniel told him the whole story. Father was so proud of Daniel and the mules that he told the story to his old friend, George Enwright. But George doubted the mules' bravery.

"Your old mules just got hungry, Roy. That's the reason they brought you and the boy home," said George.

"Well, George, you are entitled to your own opinion," answered Father. "But nothing will change my mind. In fact, I've promised Daniel that Sam and Joe can spend the rest of their days right here on the farm with us."

And so they did.

The Legend of Carcassonne

By Rosalie Maggio

Long ago, in the south of France, there was a village surrounded by high, thick walls. The people of the village raised chickens and pigs and sheep inside the village, and they raised crops on the land outside the walls.

Each night the villagers locked the huge iron gate that was the only way in or out. Safe inside the walls, they shared their food and sang songs about the noble deeds of times gone by.

King Charlemagne saw how happy the villagers were and how rich their land was. He decided to capture the village. And so one day, with much blowing of trumpets and stamping of horses' hoofs, Charlemagne and his soldiers arrived outside the village walls. Colorful tents sprouted like mushrooms as the soldiers set up camp in the nearby hills.

At first the villagers were not alarmed. Charlemagne could not get inside the walls, and the big iron gate was always locked. Once he realized he couldn't get inside, he would go away.

But Charlemagne and his soldiers did not go away. Not after a week. Not after a month. Not after a year. Charlemagne thought that sooner or later the villagers would have to come out for food.

Inside the walls, the villagers ate the fruit they had preserved the summer before. Then they ate the vegetables they had gathered in the fall. Their bags of flour began to empty, one by one.

A second year went by. The villagers planted small gardens inside the walls, but the gardens didn't produce enough food. So they ate eggs. And then they ate the chickens that laid the eggs.

Another year went by. And two more. Charlemagne and his soldiers had been camped outside the walls for five years!

Inside the walls, the villagers were thin and sad and hungry.

One day they discovered that there was nothing left to eat.

Well, not quite nothing. There was one pig left—a miserable, thin pig, to be sure, but still a pig that might make one more meal for the villagers. And someone had found a bag of wheat. The villagers gathered to divide the wheat and the skinny pig.

"And then," said one, "after we eat the last of the food, we will have to give up. We cannot hold out any longer. Charlemagne has won."

A woman named Carcas stepped forward. "No!" she said. "We will not eat the wheat. We will not eat the pig. Instead, we will feed the wheat to the pig."

A great cry went up from the villagers. What was Carcas thinking? The wheat and the pig were all that stood between them and starvation. Of course they must eat the wheat and the pig.

But Carcas repeated, "The pig shall eat the wheat." She called the others closer and whispered her plan.

And so it was that the pig found itself eating breakfast, lunch, and dinner, as well as all the snacks it wanted. True, it was wheat, wheat, and more wheat, but the pig didn't seem to mind.

When the wheat was finally gone, the villagers gathered around the gate. Opening the gate a crack, Carcas squeezed the pig through and gave it a push. Then she signaled to the girl who had been chosen to speak.

In a high-pitched voice, the girl shrieked, "Oh, Mama, I have let one of the pigs get out!"

Carcas said loudly, "Never mind, my dear. What's one pig more or less?"

Outside the walls, Charlemagne and his soldiers watched the plump little pig running and squealing around their tents. One of the soldiers grabbed the pig and brought it to Charlemagne.

Charlemagne poked the pig's fat shoulder and said, "Hmmm, even the pigs are eating well in there. In fact, this pig eats better than we do."

The soldiers shuffled their feet and grumbled. "We've been away from our homes for five years," said one. "How much longer must we stay here? They have all the food they want in there while we're eating anything we can find. I am tired of it!"

Charlemagne had to agree. The villagers seemed to have enough food to last another five years. His soldiers would never stay that long. When he nodded his head, the soldiers began pulling down the tents and saddling the horses.

Inside the gate, the villagers climbed to the tops of the high walls to watch the army retreat. As soon as Charlemagne was out of sight, Carcas ran to the village bell tower and began pulling on the heavy rope. The bells rang out over the hills.

A villager said, "Carcas *sonne.*" That is French for "Carcas is ringing the bells." And so, to this day, that is why the great walled city is called Carcassonne.

If you ever go to the south of France, you can walk along the high, thick walls of Carcassonne and remember how a clever woman—and a pig—once saved an entire village.

Crossing BIG BLUE

By Judy Cox

Jesse listened to Pa explain. "The boy's old enough, Miranda. Let him do a man's work. There's only the Big Blue crossing to worry about, and I should meet you long before that."

Jesse rocked back and forth impatiently. Pa was going to let him drive the wagon! Pa's big hand came down on his shoulder, steadying him. "Stay with the other wagons. Bo and Boo know what to do. Babe and Billy will follow. Couldn't ask for a steadier team of oxen."

Jesse knew Pa was trying to reassure Ma. She didn't want Pa to go. But the Bowen family's wagon had a broken wheel. Pa volunteered to stay behind and help Mr. Bowen fix it.

Jesse didn't give a hoot about that. He was pleased from the tip of his head right down to his toes to be driving the wagon by himself. Pa had taught him to drive during the past two weeks out from Independence. Nothing in his twelve years gave him more thrills than sitting up high above the swaying oxen, holding the thick reins between his hands.

Now he swung himself up to the seat. Pa handed him the reins. "Leave it to me, Pa," he said. Ma sat beside him. Jesse's three little sisters crowded inside. Far up the line, the wagon master gave the signal, and the train rolled west.

Jesse drove all day. The trail wound through rolling hills of grass and wild flowers. The oxen plodded along, and Ma and the girls walked. The wagon swayed like a boat on a sea of grass. Up ahead, the white covers of the wagons looked like the sails of a fleet of ships. Prairie schooners, folks called them. And Jesse was the captain.

After stopping at the nooning place, Ma and the girls climbed aboard the wagon. Jesse drove. The sky was stretched as tight as a drum, thrumming with the heat of the day. The wagon's steady pace, like the drone of insects in the grass, went on and on.

Jesse reached the Big Blue River well after the rest of the train had crossed. There was no sign of Pa. "Should we ford without him?" Ma asked anxiously. "Or should we wait?"

"It doesn't look deep," Jesse said slowly. The river glistened below them like a sleepy serpent. Across the other bank, they could make out the white covers of the other wagons, winding to the horizon. His throat was dry.

Ma looked at him. "We can wait for Pa."

"No." Jesse shook his head. "Pa said to stay with the others." His heart thudded as he drove the oxen down the hill to the bank of Big Blue.

The oxen slid a little on the red dirt of the trail. Jesse threw his whole weight against the brake to slow the wagon and keep it from turning over. They skidded downhill, shaking and rattling, until they reached the bottom. Willows and cottonwoods along the riverbank provided a cooling shade. Jesse smelled the moist, weedy river smell.

Up close, the Big Blue looked deeper and swifter than it had from the trail. The sound of rushing water filled Jesse's ears. *The other wagons crossed*, he reminded himself, swallowing hard.

"Git up!" he cried, slapping the oxen with the reins. The oxen plodded through the muddy bank and splashed into the river.

Jesse kept his eyes on Bo and Boo, the lead oxen. He didn't want to see the brown water racing past on either side. His hands gripped the reins until his knuckles turned white. The water rose up to Bo's shoulders. Ma gasped. "Git up, Bo!" Jesse called. "Steady, Boo!" The wagon creaked and Jesse saw the oxen were swimming. The water was so deep, their feet could no longer touch. *We might get swept away!* he thought in alarm.

The wagon swayed as it was lifted by the water. They were floating! The current tugged them downstream. Water ran over his knees and he could hear it rush through holes in the wagon box like water spilling through a millrace. But he dared not look. Finally, he saw the broad backs of the oxen as they clambered up the shallow side, and the wagon steadied as the wheels hit solid ground once more.

Jesse sighed. Ma reached her arm around him, and he dropped the reins and held on to her. She was crying, and he realized his eyes were wet, too. "Scared?" he said, his voice trembling a little. He patted his mother's shoulder and said as bravely as he could, "Nothing to worry about."

That night, Ma told Pa the story. By then they were camped out with the rest of the wagon train, having joined the others in time to circle the wagons. Ma had built a fire and was cooking a late dinner when Pa walked up.

The strains of a fiddle tune came from one of the wagons. But Jesse was too tired to listen. His hands hurt and his back and shoulders ached. "You did a man's work today, son," said Pa. Pa's hand on his shoulder eased some of the soreness. *A man's work*, thought Jesse happily. He stifled a yawn. He'd done a man's work. But he was awfully glad Pa was back!

Freedom Day

By Joan Strauss

"Today's going to be like Christmas!" Jamie said as she opened her eyes on this November morning in 1849.

"Today is the freedom day!" her brothers and sisters shouted happily at her as she came into the kitchen for breakfast.

Jamie was not sure what freedom meant. She knew only that her family, like all the other slaves on the island of St. Thomas in the West Indies, would be freed today.

Still, she laughed when one of her little brothers asked, "When does the freedom come? Can I see it when it comes?"

Jamie's pa turned from where he was sitting in the cabin doorway and said, "We don't belong to the plantation anymore. We belong to ourselves. Nobody can buy us or sell us. We can do what we want, as long as it doesn't harm other folks. This is what the freedom is, and I don't want any of you to forget it."

Mama had tears in her eyes, but she was laughing. "We should give thanks to the Lord right this minute for bringing us this day," she said.

The family, their laughter stilled, obeyed. The silence did not last long. The sound of firecrackers sent the children racing from the house as soon as their father uttered the "Amen."

Jamie met her friends to join the celebration downtown in Charlotte Amalie. People, dressed in their best, were singing and dancing in the streets. Music twanged from all kinds of homemade instruments. Exploding firecrackers added to the din.

Finally, tired of running with the crowds, the children reached their favorite spot at the waterfront. From the stones piled high there, they liked to watch the schooners arrive and unload their cargoes or set sail with the tide.

They often played pirate. They would mount the rocks and gaze out at the harbor, firing imaginary cannons and capturing imaginary ships. Sometimes, they could persuade an idle sailor to tell them marvelous tales of his adventures at sea.

Today, the docks were completely deserted. Jamie went home to the holiday meal her mother had promised.

When her father blessed the food, Jamie was puzzled by his closing words: "And help us find a way to build our church."

"Why do we need a church, Pa?" Jamie asked. "We have a church."

"Yes, a whitewashed wooden shack. That's not a church for free people. We may be poor, but we should give God the best church our hands can build."

"It's not the kind of church, James, that's important," Jamie's mother said to her husband. "It's what's in our hearts when we pray."

Jamie's father agreed. "I know that, Mary. But we want a church so beautiful, we will never forget where our freedom and other blessings come from. Some of our friends and neighbors are meeting here this afternoon to make plans."

Later, Jamie sat quietly in a corner while people from the plantation filed into the little cabin. She listened carefully while they talked of constructing a real church.

"A church like that means a lot of things," one man warned. "We need pews and an altar."

"And windows made of glass," added another.

"We want a fine door, too."

"We want no house of wood," Jamie's father declared. "This church should be of stone."

"Stone?" exclaimed an older man. "You are a dreamer! How will we find enough money for all those things?"

Jamie jumped up. "I know where there's stone, lots of it!" She shrank back into her corner, frightened by her boldness, as all the men turned to her.

"What do you mean, girl?" asked the old man.

Jamie wished she could hide behind her father, but the old man dragged her out of the corner. "What do you mean?"

"The big stones near the wharf. The sailors said they were used for ballast in the trading ships that used to come here." Jamie was too shy to say more. She hoped her father would understand what she was trying to tell them.

"Jamie is right." Her father did understand. "Those piles of stones at the waterfront don't belong to anybody, as far as I know. They have been there as long as I can remember."

With her father's hand resting on her shoulder, Jamie felt brave enough to explain. "It was a long time ago, maybe a hundred years ago. The sailors say St. Thomas was part of Denmark then instead of England, the way we are now."

"Ha ha!" cackled the old man. "That's a smart girl you have there, James. You'd better send her to that new school they're talking about."

"I hope to," answered Jamie's father.

Jamie could hardly speak for her excitement. Plantation girls never went to school! It looked as if things were going to be different with freedom.

They were waiting for her to go on. She took a deep breath. "The ships came from Denmark for our sugar. The sailors filled the holds with heavy stones to balance the empty ships on the way over. Then they dumped the stones on the shore to make room for the sugar."

"The girl's got a good idea!"

"Maybe we could use those rocks!"

"It would be good to clear them away!"

A hubbub broke out as all the men talked at once. Jamie edged her way along the wall to the door and slipped out unnoticed into the sun-filled afternoon. The celebration was still going strong in town. All sorts of adventures might be waiting for her.

But years later, whenever Jamie passed the big stone church, which still stands in Charlotte Amalie, she remembered the look of pride on her father's face more than all the adventures of that freedom day.

The Necklace

By Anne Schraff

"Come along, Nathan," Father said, raising the pack to his back. Nathan hoisted his own pack and followed his father down the dirt path. It was the Ohio valley in 1800, and Nathan and his father were peddlers. They bought supplies at the wholesale house, then sold them at farmhouses in the wilderness.

Nathan's father carried calico cloth, ribbons, bows, and clothing in his pack. Nathan carried lighter items, such as needles, thread, and jewelry.

There was one item in Nathan's pack that he didn't want to sell. It was a beautiful sparkly necklace. He wanted to give it to his little sister, Rachel, for her birthday. Father said if the necklace did not sell this trip, Rachel could have it.

At each farmhouse where Nathan and his father stopped that morning, they opened their packs and sold cloth and bows, but nobody bought the necklace. Nathan was happy about that. Rachel had been very sick this past winter, and she was pale and weak. Nathan thought a necklace that shone with the fire of the sun would bring a glow of happiness to her cheeks.

Up ahead there was another farmhouse. "We can stop there before we eat," Father said.

A woman came to the door. "Oh, good! Margaret, the peddlers are here!" she called. A girl about eighteen hurried into the room as Nathan and his father opened their packs.

"Look!" the woman cried in excitement. "The calico cloth is beautiful. It has wonderful designs!"

Margaret held some horn combs to her long, dark hair and said, "Mother, are these pretty?"

Nathan hoped she wouldn't see the necklace, but she did.

"Oh!" cried Margaret. "I must have this necklace!"

Nathan's heart sank. There were earrings in his

pack as well. "These are such pretty earrings. Wouldn't you like these instead?" he asked Margaret.

"No!" she snapped. "I want the necklace!"

"Oh, very well, Margaret," sighed her mother. The woman turned to Nathan's father and said, "We'll buy the necklace and six yards of the calico."

Nathan tugged at his father's sleeve. "It's Rachel's necklace, Father," he whispered.

Father looked at Nathan and frowned. "We need money for the whole family. I must sell the necklace if there is someone to buy it," he said.

As Nathan and his father walked from the house, Father put his arm around Nathan's shoulders. "Don't worry, son. We'll give Rachel a beautiful bow." Nathan nodded, but he knew she would have been happier with the necklace.

The two of them found a small creek. They sat beside it and ate lunch.

Suddenly an idea came to Nathan. "Father, I think I may have left something there," he said.

"All right," Father said. "I'll wait right here."

Nathan ran as fast as he could back to the farmhouse. When he knocked on the door, the woman appeared. "Why, it's the peddler's son," she said.

Nathan swallowed and took from his pocket the most valuable possession he owned, a fine knife. "I have a little sister who has been very sick," he began. "I wanted to cheer her by giving her the necklace you bought for your daughter. But if you choose the earrings instead, I would give you my knife besides . . . It would be a fine deal."

The woman studied the knife. "It's a fine knife indeed. Worth much more than the necklace. And you would give us this and the earrings as well if we returned the necklace?" she asked.

"Yes," Nathan said. He opened his pack and took out the earrings.

"To meet a boy like you touches my heart, young man. Give me the earrings and knife and I will give you back the necklace."

"Thank you," Nathan said with a big smile. As he walked away, the woman patted his pack and waved. When he returned to his father, he told him what he'd done. His father just smiled and shook his head. "It seems to me," he said, "that woman got a good deal, but it was a fine thing for you to do, son."

"It will surely make Rachel happy," Nathan added, reaching into his pack to take out the necklace. As his hand closed around it, he felt something else in the bottom of his pack. It was smooth and familiar to touch—his knife! The woman had returned it to him. Nathan looked back at the little farmhouse and blessed her.

Magic Medicine

By Kathy Millhoff

Caro Garrett stopped and stared at the square whitewashed building that served as the town's medical clinic, then she slowly climbed the steps to the door. *If I weren't the doctor's daughter,* she thought to herself, *I'd be at the mercantile with Hannah, eating molasses drops.*

"But no sense wishing for what can't be," Caro said aloud. She opened the heavy wooden door and called, "Father? I'm home."

There was no answer, and Caro realized that she would be spending yet another afternoon alone, tending clinic for her father.

With a heavy sigh, she dropped her gray canvas schoolbag onto a bench inside the door and went to the back of the room. There, she shoved aside a curtain and climbed the steep wooden stairway to her home above.

She found her father's note on the scrubbed pine kitchen table. It read:

Carolina,

Tend clinic and lock up at sunset. I shall be at the Sawyer ranch seeing to a compound fracture.

Father

Caro crumpled the paper and tossed it into the now cold wood-burning stove. Quickly, she changed into her old dress and put on a white apron. She smoothed her windblown hair with her hands. That, she decided, would have to do.

She hoped it wouldn't be long before she could travel to boarding school in the East. She was tired of Wyoming, with its huge empty spaces and long, lonely hours of work.

Now, sitting in the window seat in the clinic, she stared at puffy clouds in the high blue sky and wished for the thousandth time that her father was not the town doctor. Her swinging foot caught the strap of her book bag on the neighboring bench and sent it thudding to the floor. The sound of books hitting the floor reminded her of end-of-term examinations.

"More maps!" she grumbled, giving the bag an extra kick. "Twisting rivers . . . and far-off countries!"

Her words trailed off as she spotted Hannah and Delia walking arm in arm from the mercantile, each with her own lemon stick.

"Hannah! Dee!" Caro shouted as she knocked on the glass. But the rumble of a heavy freight wagon must have drowned out her voice, because the girls turned in another direction. Caro sighed.

That Thursday afternoon was particularly dull. Not one person glanced in the direction of the clinic. Though she should have been glad to have quiet to study, she also liked answering patient's questions. Medicines were locked up when her father was away, but she often offered advice or throat paint.

After locking and shuttering the clinic at sunset, Caro climbed back upstairs and lit the oil lamp.

"Well, I wonder what there is to eat for supper," she spoke out loud. She rummaged around the fruit bin in the pantry and found a juicy apple. Crunching into the fruit, she picked up a book, lit a lamp, and opened her mathematics book. Soon, tiredness took over and she went to bed.

She awoke with a start. Hard rain was making a loud *ping ping pa-ting ping* on the tin roof, and she thought the storm had awakened her.

"Another storm from the mountains," she told herself, snuggling down to go back to sleep. Then she heard banging on the clinic door.

Father! she thought, throwing on her dress and grabbing the lamp.

She held the lamp high as she opened the door to see Sam Kendall, her classmate. He stumbled in, banging the door behind him to shut out the howling wind and rain.

"Where's the doc?" he shouted.

"Not here. What's wrong?"

"It's my sister, Abbey. Something's made her terribly sick."

Caro remembered the tiny, freckle-faced redhead tagging after Sam on days when the Kendalls came to town.

"What's wrong?" Caro asked.

"She's very hot and covered with spots."

Caro felt cold fear now. If it was smallpox, they were all in trouble.

But then she calmed and said, "Measles, probably. Isn't your mother with her?"

"They've gone to Laramie for a couple of days."

"I'll come back with you, then."

"I need your father."

"The doctor won't be back tonight," Caro interrupted with self-importance.

She wrapped a shawl around her shoulders, jammed her feet into boots, and led Sam to where tired old Beulah waited patiently.

"I hope she'll carry us both," Sam grumbled.

"She will," Caro assured him, climbing up.

After what seemed like hours of winding trails, the horse finally reached the Kendall barn. Caro slid to the ground and stumbled to the cabin.

She hung her dripping shawl on a peg beside the door and looked around the room. Abbey lay in a trundle bed, her tangled hair clinging to her flushed cheeks.

"Hello, Abbey," Caro said. "Time to braid that pretty hair."

Caro combed out and braided Abbey's hair and for the next several hours worked with Sam to cool down her fever. She drizzled honey into warm water and made Abbey sip as much as she could. She dipped a cloth into cool water and wiped the little girl's face and neck. Sam brought in fresh water and made sure the fire was warm and bright as Caro talked or sang to Abbey.

It was in the middle of "Sweet Betsy from Pike" that she noticed Abbey had dropped off to sleep. Sam was slumped against the woodpile, snoring softly. Slowly, Caro felt her own eyelids droop.

"More magic medicine, please," a child's voice cut through Caro's dreams. She blinked, then she saw her father standing beside Abbey's bed.

"Father," she mumbled, "is it measles?"

"It is," he replied. "You have had them, so there is no fear of contagion."

"Father, I wasn't sure. . . ."

Caro looked at Abbey, whose rash remained, but who looked better and happier than she had before.

"You did well, Caro, though it was young Kendall who left the note saying where you'd be."

"Caro, I want more magic medicine," Abbey repeated her request.

"I don't understand," Caro said.

"It's the healer's touch," her father said. "There is often more healing in a calm voice and soothing touch than in a medicine. Every doctor knows that."

"We missed the examinations," Sam said, carrying in yet more water.

"Oh no," Caro groaned.

Dr. Garrett looked up from where he was wrapping Abbey in a patchwork quilt.

"This time," he said, "doctoring was more important than schoolwork. But I am sure I can work out arrangements with Miss Thorncroft."

"Will we have magic medicine at the clinic?" Abbey asked.

"There's lots of magic medicine there," Caro assured her.

Caro was so pleased with her father's praise that she felt as though she had had a little magic medicine herself.

Save Savannah!

By Marcella Fisher Anderson

Henny climbed to a branch near the top of the live oak, where he carved the date: December 19, 1864. Then he looked across the salt marshes toward unusual noises on the Savannah River. He walked toward them, reaching a Confederate encampment before noon.

"Hey there, Henny," said the officer of the guard who knew him. "Them Yankees are coming."

"I know that, sir," Henny said. "The marshes are fillin' up with land critters. Crows flew in yesterday, and I've seen woodchucks, too."

The officer rubbed his eyes. "Seems after burning Atlanta, the Yankees are burning their way to our beautiful Savannah."

Henny felt hot with anger. "What's General Hardee doin' about it?"

"General Hardee has been ordered not to defend Savannah, so that the city will not be burned. See there? We're building a pontoon bridge across the river now to head north to South Carolina. Keep a lookout for the Yankee scouts, Henny. They may be in the marshes by late tomorrow."

As the saltwater tide came in, Henny returned to his own campsite. The marsh seemed too quiet. He could hear the clicking of feeding oysters clinging to the mangrove roots and reached down to pluck off a few for his supper.

Henny hadn't always lived in the marsh, but it had been his father's favorite place. The day Henny read his father's name listed among the dead on the posted casualty list, he ran away from home. He never even stopped to say good-bye to his Gramma Peaches. Henny ran and ran until he came to the river and couldn't run any farther. Then he sat down beneath a swamp oak and cried. Finally, when he stopped, it was so quiet in the marsh—so peaceful—that he decided to stay for a short spell. That was months ago.

Suddenly, Henny stopped short. Right in front of him lay a shuddering body dressed in dark blue. A cap with a shiny visor lay on the ground beside him along with a rifle. A short distance away crouched an alligator, all ten feet of it, still as a stone monument. Not even its yellow-rimmed eyes blinked.

"Stand up," said Henny softly to the lying figure. "Find your feet, Yankee boy."

Swiftly, the young scout stood.

"Now stay stood. Old Yeller Eyes won't attack nothin' that's towerin' over him. Don't stir 'til he's good and gone."

While the tide lapped softly, Old Yeller Eyes moved its head and turned around with a slow, dragging twist of its body, then splashed into the water.

Wordlessly, the young Yankee followed Henny to his fire. "You can stop shakin' now," said Henny, stirring the embers. "Old Yeller Eyes almost got ya—trompin' through his territory, stirrin' things up. It's no wonder."

"I thought if I lay on the ground, I could watch him better."

"You mean he could watch you better. Shows how much you Yankees know. If we Rebs don't git ya, the wildlife will. Warm yourself now." He stopped to think for a moment. "When you catch up with your scoutin' friends, tell them Savannah is nowhere near here."

"I reckon I owe you a 'thank you,' Johnny Reb."

"I reckon ya do. Now I'll thank you to git out of here—all you Yankees—before I send Old Yeller Eyes and his friends lookin' for you." Without another word, the Yankee soldier disappeared into the swampy woods.

The marsh seemed alive with intruders. Alarmed, the great blue heron rose from the water, its long, thin legs dangling.

Henny ran back to warn General Hardee's encampment. It seemed that the Yankees hadn't waited for tomorrow.

Throughout the next day, Henny watched Hardee's men hurriedly set the flat-bottomed boats in place, lay down wood flats, then cover the bridge with rice straw to muffle the thousands of wagon wheels and soldiers marching across in broken quick step.

When the last of General Hardee's army had slipped away in the night, there was a loneliness in the marsh. Henny sat by his fire with his chin on his knees. A thin coating of ice clung to the broom grasses; winter was coming. The marsh didn't seem to belong to Henny anymore, what with all the strangers trekking through it. Oddest of all, he realized that, for the first time in many weeks, he had cared about other people. He was glad he had warned the young Yankee.

The thought of Christmas tugged at his heart. Even during these war years, Gramma Peaches could make something of the day. Besides, he still had a sack of black walnuts he'd picked for her.

Before dawn, he made up his mind that he wouldn't spend another night in the marsh. The eastern sky was clear as he walked the road to Savannah and reached a small rise. Below lay the city—ablaze with light. For a terrible moment, Henny thought Savannah was burning. But it was only the red sun rising on the Customs House, the churches, and the white marble fountains in the squares. A smile crossed Henny's thin face.

As he entered the city, he avoided the Yankee soldiers handing out food to the people on the streets. He paused outside a small house hung with Spanish moss. He knew that inside Gramma Peaches would greet him with a hug and say, "I knew you'd be home for Christmas, Henny dear. You and Savannah—both saved."

Still, Henny waited, holding the sack of walnuts, until somehow he could hear from far away the hard flap of the heron's wings.

Stagecoach Ride

By Anne Schraff

"Are you sure you won't mind riding the stagecoach to visit Uncle Quentin and Aunt Rose, Eve?" Father asked.

"You're only ten years old," Mother said, "and you'll be taking the trip alone."

"I'll be fine," Eve insisted. It was 1860 in California. Uncle Quentin and Aunt Rose were Eve's favorite relatives. Uncle Quentin took her up into the mountains to camp and fish. Aunt Rose let her cut fabric squares for her very own patchwork quilt.

"I wish I could go with you," Father said, "but I can't get away from my work."

"The new baby needs me, or I'd go with you," Mother said.

"I can go alone," Eve said. "It'll be fun." She was excited about riding a stagecoach across the hills and desert to the ranch at the foot of the high, rugged mountains.

Early the next morning, Father took Eve to the stage depot. The sun was coming up like a fiery ball, and already it was hot.

"Here comes the stage," Father said.

Eve turned her head quickly and saw four horses racing out of a cloud of dust. The coach was red and gold with flowers and vines painted on the side. This would be Eve's first ride in a stagecoach.

The driver sat way up high, but he jumped down easily. He grabbed Eve's bag and stuffed it into a compartment under his seat. "Now remember, folks," he said to the passengers. "Don't spit against the wind. Don't complain about the food at the next depot. We do the best we can. And no smelly pipes inside the coach!"

Eve felt her body tingle with excitement. She couldn't wait for the trip to begin.

"Have a good time," Father said, giving Eve a hug. She climbed inside and waved to her father from the window. With a jolt, the coach raced away. The horses leaped forward so fast that Eve almost fell on the floor. A red-bearded man across from her caught her. Eve's face turned red.

"Ever ride in a stagecoach before, miss?" asked the red-bearded man.

"No," Eve said.

"It's no picnic," laughed the man. In the next minute the stagecoach hit something in the road. Eve bounced from her seat and almost hit the ceiling. "I guess we hit a big rock," she said breathlessly.

"Nope," said the red-bearded man, "more likely we hit a pebble. This is like riding a bucking bronco the whole way."

As they moved along, Eve hung on tightly. When the coach turned, all the passengers slid against the window. They were squeezed together like sardines in a can.

Then a man rode by and fired a rifle into the air.

"Whoa! Whoa!" screamed the driver as the horses galloped out of control.

"Runaway horses!" one of the passengers screamed. "We better jump out! This stagecoach is going to roll over!"

"Hold on, fellow," cried the red-bearded man. "If you jump out you'll break your neck. We've got a smart driver. He'll get control of the horses."

Eve was so scared she held her breath. It seemed the horses were galloping wildly for a long time. She could hear the shouts of the driver and rider as they tried to slow the horses. Finally the coach slowed and Eve let out her breath with a *whoosh.*

"You're white as a ghost," the red-bearded man told Eve. She didn't say a word. She had never been so scared in her life.

It got hotter in the coach as the sun rose in the late-morning sky. It was like the inside of an oven. When the coach stopped for the noon meal, Eve was glad to get out. Her legs were rubbery. She almost stumbled when she stepped down from the stage.

Everybody lined up at the wash basin to wash the dust off their hands and faces and to take a drink of water. "Hurry up, hurry up, don't lag there," said the driver. "We have to move along."

Eve bought a sandwich, but the bread was hard as a board and the meat tasted like a piece of old boot leather. Her stomach growled with hunger, but she couldn't eat the lunch.

Eve climbed back on the stage. She ached all over, and she began bouncing around again as the coach hit small ruts in the road. She was hungry and thirsty and hot.

Then, at last, Eve saw her stop in the distance. Uncle Quentin stood waiting for her. The coach ground to a halt, and the driver jumped down and opened the door for her. Uncle Quentin pulled her bag from under the driver's seat and gave her a great bear hug.

"How was the trip, Eve?" Uncle Quentin asked with a grin.

Dust coated Eve's hair and clothing. Even her lips and tongue were dusty. But she flashed a big dusty smile and said, "It was great, Uncle Quentin. It was fun!"